Beowulf

Adapted by Henriette Barkow
Illustrated by Alan Down

Arabic translation by Dr Sajida Fawzi

MANTRA

Tale of GRendel,
creatures
ch Terrible MMonsrtosity
and Eviel

And so The GReat HER
BEownlf son Of the M
o fTHE massiev te
SLAyer

هل سمعت هذا القول؟

يقولون أنه فى الوقت الذى يكون فيه الكثير من الكلام والضحك فإن غرندِل يأتى ويأخذك بعيداً عن هذا الجو. أنت لا تعرف شيئاً عن غرندِل؟

ولِذا فأنا أعتقد أنك لا تعرف شيئاً عن بيُولف أيضاً. إستمع بإصغاء فسوف أقصُّ عليك قصة أعظم محارب من الغيتس وكيف قاتل الوحش الشرّير غرندِل.

Did you hear that?

They say that if there is too much talking and laughter, Grendel will come and drag you away. You don't know about Grendel? Then I suppose you don't know about Beowulf either. Listen closely and I will tell you the story of the greatest Geat warrior and how he fought the vile monster, Grendel.

منذ أكثر من ألف سنة قرّر الملك الدانماركي روثكار بناء بلاط كبير للإحتفال بانتصارات محاربيه المخلصين. وعندما تمّ بناء البلاط أسماه هيروت وأعلن أنه سيُخصص للإحتفالات وتقديم الهبات. وكان بلاط هيروت يقف مرتفعاً ومطلاً على مساحة من أراضى المستنقعات المقفرة. ويمكن رُؤية جملون البناية الناصع البياض من مسافة أميال.

More than a thousand years ago the Danish King Hrothgar decided to build a great hall to celebrate the victories of his loyal warriors. When the hall was finished he named it Heorot and proclaimed that it should be a place for feasting, and for the bestowing of gifts. Heorot towered over the desolate marshy landscape. Its white gables could be seen for miles.

وفى ليلة سوداء مظلمة أقام روثكار أوّل حفل كبير له فى هذا البلاط وقدّم للمحاربين وزوجاتهم أرقى أنواع الطعام والشراب. وحضرها أيضاً المغنّين والموسيقيين.

On a dark and moonless night Hrothgar held his first great banquet in the main hall. There was the finest food and ale for all the warriors and their wives. There were minstrels and musicians too.

ويُمكن أن تسمَع أصواتهم المبتهجة عَبرَ المستنقعات وحتى المياه الزرقاء
الداكنة حيث يعيش هناك وحش شرّير.
إنه غرندِل الذي كان فيما مضى إنساناً ولكنه وحش دموى قاسٍ الآن.
وبالرغم من أنه لم يَعُد إنساناً إلا أنه لا زال يحتفظ ببعض السمات الإنسانية.

Their joyous sounds could be heard all across the marshes to the dark
blue waters, where an evil being lived.
Grendel - once a human, but now a cruel and bloodthirsty creature.
Grendel - no longer a man, but still with some human features.

غضب غرندِل كثيراً حين سمع الأصوات المبتهجة القادمة من البلاط، وفى وقت متأخر
من تلك الليلة، وعندما استأذن الملك والملكة وذهبا الى غرفتهما وعندما كان كل المحاربين
نائمين، تسلل غرندِل عِبرَ المستنقعات الوحلة. وعندما وصل الباب وجدها مقفلة ولكن
بدفعة قويّة واحدة استطاع فتح الباب والدخول.

Grendel was much angered by the sounds of merriment that came from the hall.
Late that night, when the king and queen had retired to their rooms, and all the
warriors were asleep, Grendel crept across the squelching marshes. When he reached
the door he found it barred. With one mighty blow he pushed the door open. Then
Grendel was inside.

وفى تلك الليلة قتل غرندِل فى قاعة البلاط ثلاثين من أشجع محاربى الملك روثكار. قطع
أعناقهم بيديه المخلبيّتين وشرب دمهم قبل أن ينهش لحمهم بأسنانه. وعندما قضى عليهم
جميعاً عاد غرندِل الى بيته الرطب المعتم تحت الموجات المائية.

That night, in that hall, Grendel slaughtered thirty of Hrothgar's bravest warriors.
He snapped their necks with his claw like hands, and drank their blood, before
sinking his teeth into their flesh. When none were left alive Grendel returned to his
dark dank home beneath the watery waves.

وفى الصباح امتلأت قاعة البلاط حزناً وبكاءً.
فإن مشهد أقوى وأشجع الدانماركيين ملأ الأرض حزناً ويأساً عميقاً.
واستمر غرندِل ولمدة إثنى عشر شتاءً يهاجم ويقتل كل من يقترب من بلاط هيروت.
وقد حاول عدد من شجعان القبيلة قتال غرندِل ولكن قوتهم لم تستطع الوقوف بوجه
هذا الشرير.

In the morning the hall was filled with weeping and grieving. The sight of the carnage of the strongest and bravest Danes filled the land with a deep despairing sadness.

For twelve long winters Grendel continued to ravage and kill any who came near Heorot. Many a brave clansman tried to do battle with Grendel, but their armour was useless against the evil one.

وانتشرت كثيراً وبعيداً قصص غرندِل وأعماله الشريرة. وأخيراً وصلت هذه القصص الى
بيُولف، أقوى وأنبل محارب فى قبيلته، وأقسَمَ بان يقتل الوحش الشرير.

The stories of the terrible deeds of Grendel were carried far and wide.
Eventually they reached Beowulf, the mightiest and noblest warrior of his people.
He vowed that he would slay the evil monster.

أبحر بيُولف إلى السواحل الدانماركية مع أربعة عشر من رجاله الأقوياء المخلصين.
وعندما وصلوا اعترضهم حرّاس السواحل قائلين "لِيَقِف كل من يقصد النزول!
ما غرضكم من القدوم إلى هذه السواحل؟"
وأجاب بيُولف قائلاً "أنا بيُولف. ركبت المصاعب وقصدت بلدكم لمحاربة غرندِل
لأجل روثكار مَلِكِكُم. وأمرهم قائلاً أسرعوا وخذونى اليه."

Beowulf sailed with fourteen of his loyal thanes to the Danish shore. As they landed the coastal guards challenged them: "Halt he who dares to land! What is thy calling upon these shores?"

"I am Beowulf. I have ventured to your lands to fight Grendel for your king, Hrothgar. So make haste and take me to him," he commanded.

وصل بيُولف الى بلاط هيروت وتَفقَد الأرض المقفرة حوله حيث يعيش غرندِل فى مكان ما هناك ثُمَ دخل قاعة هيروت بعزم وتصميم.

Beowulf arrived at Heorot and surveyed the desolate landscape. Grendel was somewhere out there. With resolve in his heart he turned and entered the hall.

قدّم بيُولف نفسه الى الملك قائلاً "إنك أنت الملك الحق. النبيل للدانماركيين. هذا وعدى أقطعه لك: سأخلصكم من الشرير غرندِل."

أجاب الملك قائلاً "لقد سمعت من أعمالك الشجاعة وقوتك الجبارة ولكن غرندِل أقوى من أي مخلوق واجهته."

ولكن بيُولف طمأن الملك وأكّد له قائلاً "روثكار، ليس فقط سأقتل غرندِل وأتغلّب عليه بل سأفعل ذلك بيدىَّ المجرّدتين." واعتقد الكثيرون أن ذلك كان كلاماً هُراءً حيث أنهم لم يسمعوا عن أعماله الشجاعة وقوته الجبارة.

Beowulf presented himself to the king. "Hrothgar, true and noble King of the Danes, this is my pledge: I will rid thee of the evil Grendel."

"Beowulf, I have heard of your brave deeds and great strength but Grendel is stronger than any living being that you would ever have encountered," replied the king.

"Hrothgar, I will not only fight and defeat Grendel, but I will do it with my bare hands," Beowulf assured the king.
Many thought that this was an idle boast, for they had not heard of his great strength and brave deeds.

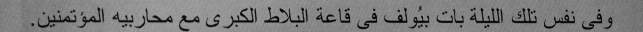

وفى نفس تلك الليلة بات بيُولف فى قاعة البلاط الكبرى مع محاربيه المؤتمنين.

That very night Beowulf and his most trusted warriors
lay down to sleep in the great hall.

وعندما أظلم الوقت اتّجه غرندِل الى قاعة البلاط عِبْرَ المستنقعات دون أن يُدرك أنه
لن يتمكن من أن يرويَ تعطشه للدم هذه الليلة.
دفع غرندِل بنفسه بقوة إلى داخل قاعة البلاط. سحب احد المحاربين من مقعدة بشدة
وقصم رقبته وشرب دمه ورماه جانباً.

As the light dimmed, Grendel made his way across the
marshy ground to the hall not realising that tonight
his bloodthirsty cravings would not be satisfied.
    Grendel burst into the hall.
He wrenched a warrior from
his bench, snapped his neck
and drank his blood,
and then tossed
him aside.

واتّجه الى المقعد التالى وسحب بشدة الرجل الذى كان جالساً عليه.
وعندما تحسّس قبضة بيُولف أدرك أنه يواجه قوّة عظيمة كقوّته.

He moved on to the next bench and grabbed that man. When he felt
Beowulf's grip he knew that he had met a power as great as his own.

صاح به بيُولف قائلاً "كفى، أيها الوحش الشرير!"
"سوف أقاتلك حتى الموت، وسوف يسُود الخير."
تقدّم غرندِل إلى الأمام ليمسك بحنجرة المحارب ولكن بيُولف قبض على ساعده.
واشتبك الإثنان فى قتال فتّاك فقد كان كل منهما فى غاية التأهّب والإستعداد للقضاء
على الآخر. وأخيراً باستعمال كلّ ما لديه من قوّة تمكن بيُولف من أن يشُقَّ ساعد
غرندِل ويقطعها.

"No more, you evil being!" commanded Beowulf. "I shall fight you to the death.
Good shall prevail."

Grendel lunged forward to grab the warrior's throat but Beowulf grabbed his arm.
Thus they were locked in mortal combat. Each was seething with the desire to kill the
other. Finally, with a mighty jerk, and using all the power within him, Beowulf ripped
Grendel's arm off.

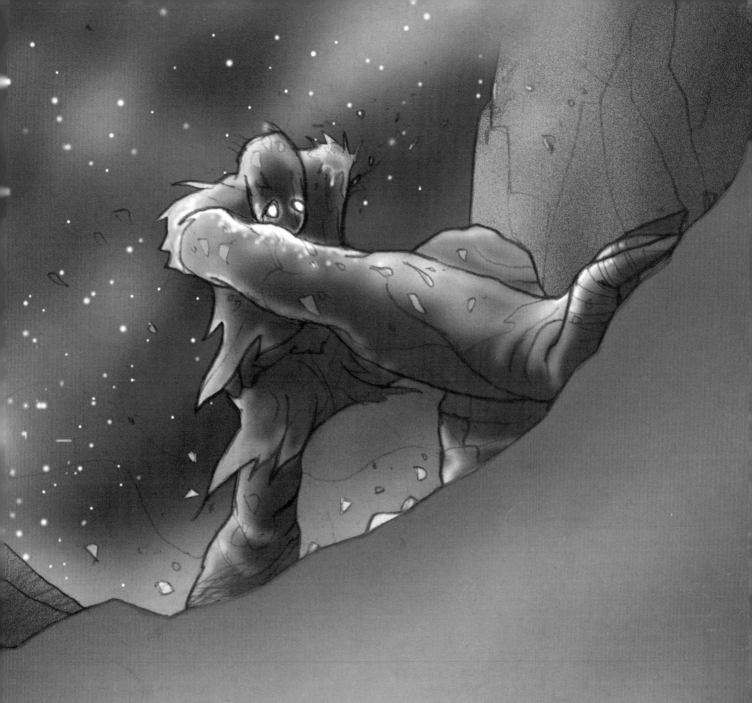

صراخ مرعب شقّ سكون الليل عندما خرج غرندِل مترنّحاً متأثراً بجراحه تاركاً خلفه آثار قطرات من الدم. وسار للمرة الأخيرة عِبْرَ المستنقعات المضبّبة ثمّ مات فى كهفه هناك تحت الماء الدرك الداكن.

A terrible scream pierced the night air as Grendel staggered away, leaving a trail of blood. He crossed the misty marshes for the last time, and died in his cave beneath the dark blue murky waters.

رفع بيُولف فوق رأسة ساعد غرندِل حتى يراها الجميع وصاح منادياً "أنا، بيُولف لقد انتصرت على غرندِل. فقد انتصر الخير على الشرّ!"

وعندما قدّم بيُولف ساعد غرندِل إلى الملك روثكار ابتهج الملك وقدّم الشكر له قائلاً "يُولف، يا أعظم الرجال، من الآن فصاعداً سيكون حبى لكَ كحب أبٍ لإبنه وسأهبك مالاً كثيراً."

وجرى احتفال كبير فى تلك الليلة بمناسبة انتصار بيُولف على عدو روثكار.

ولكن يبدو أن هذا الإبتهاج جاء مبكراً.

Beowulf lifted the arm above his head for all to see and proclaimed: "I, Beowulf have defeated Grendel. Good has triumphed over evil!"

When Beowulf presented Hrothgar with Grendel's arm the king rejoiced and gave his thanks: "Beowulf, greatest of men, from this day forth I will love thee like a son and bestow wealth upon you."

A great feast was commanded for that night to celebrate Beowulf's defeat of Hrothgar's enemy.

But the rejoicing came too soon.

تحت ذلك الماء البارد الداكن كان هناك أمّ حزينة على ابنها.
أم أقسمت على الإنتقام ممّن سبّب موته. وفى منتصف الليل قطعت سطح الماء سباحة
ووصلت إلى قاعة بلاط هيروت. فأفزعت وأرعبت الذين كانوا هناك.
سحبت بقوة أحد محاربى الملك روثكار، قصمت رقبته وأسرعت به
إلى الخارج لتلتهمه فى هدوء.

لقد نسى الجميع أن غرندِل له أمّ.

Under the deep blue chilling waters a mother mourned her
son and vowed to avenge his death. In the middle of the
night, she swam to the surface and made the journey to
the hall of Heorot. Here she terrorised those within.
She grabbed one of Hrothgar's warriors, wrung
his neck and ran off to devour him in peace.

All had forgotten that Grendel had a mother.

مرة أخرى امتلأت قاعة بلاط هيروت بأصوات الحزن بل وبأصوات الغضب أيضاً.
وقام روثكار باستدعاء بيُولف ومرة أُخرى تعّهد بيُولف بالقتال قائلاً "سأتغلب على
أم غرندِل. إنّ القتل يجب أنْ ينتهى ويتوقف."
وبعد أن انتهى من كلامه هذا جمع محاربيه الأربعة عشر النبلاء وامتطوا خيولهم
متوجهين إلى المستنقع الذى يعيش به غرندِل.

Once more Heorot was filled with the sound of mourning, but also of anger.
Hrothgar summoned Beowulf to his chamber, and once more Beowulf pledged
to do battle: "I will go and defeat Grendel's mother. The killing has to stop." With
these words he gathered his fourteen noble warriors and rode out towards Grendel's
watery home.

تَتَبّعوا مَسار الوحش الشرير عَبْرَ المستنقعات حتى وصلوا الى جرف على الساحل وهناك وقعت عيونهم على مَشهد مُرعب : وجدوا رأس المحارب المقتول مُعلّق على شجرة بجانبها مياه ملطّخة بالدماء.

They tracked the monster across the marshes until they reached some cliffs. There a terrible sight met their eyes: the head of the slain warrior hanging from a tree by the side of the blood stained waters.

ترجّل بيُولف عن حصانه ولبس درعه وغاص فى الماء العكر وسيفه بيده. وبعد ساعات من الغوص فى أعماق الماء، وصل إلى القعر وهناك وجد نفسه وجهاً لوجه مع أُم غرندِل.

Beowulf dismounted from his horse and put on his armour. With sword in hand he plunged into the gloomy water. Down and down he swam until after many an hour he reached the bottom. There, he came face to face with Grendel's mother.

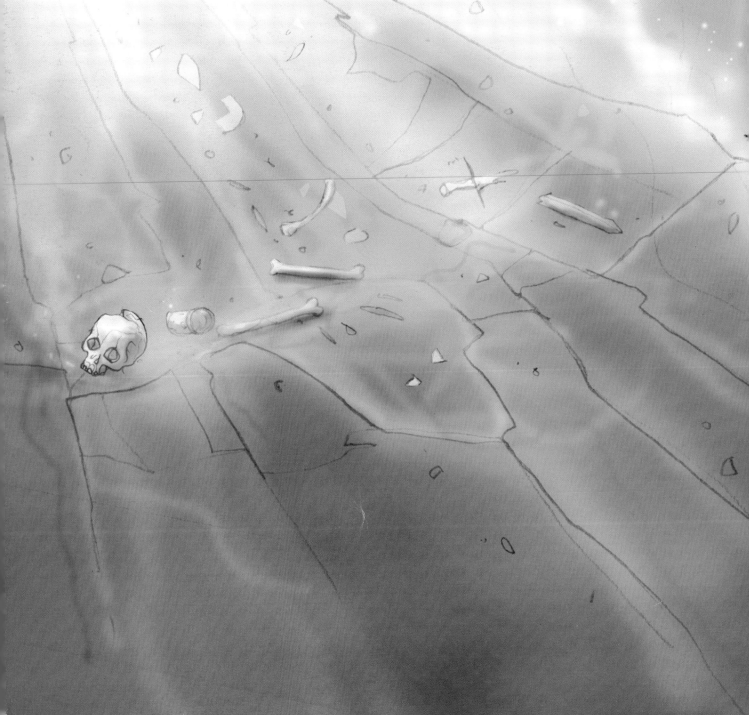

هاجمته أُم غرندِل وسحبته بمخالبها إلى كهفها ولولا درعه لقَضت عليه.

She lunged at him, and clutching him with her claws, she dragged him into her cave. If it had not been for his armour he would surely have perished.

وهناك فى الكهف سحب بيُولف سيفه وضربها بقوة على رأسها ولكنها لم تكن ضربة نافذة ولم تترك أى أثر. رمى سيفه بعيداً وقبض عليها من أكتافها ورماها أرضاً. أوو، ولكن بيُولف تعثّر فى تلك اللحظة، وسحبت الوحشة الشريرة خنجرها وطعنته.

Within the cavern Beowulf drew his sword, and with a mighty blow struck her on the head. But the sword skimmed off and left no mark. Beowulf slung his sword away. He seized the monster by the shoulders and threw her to the ground. Oh, but at that moment Beowulf tripped, and the evil monster drew her dagger and stabbed him.

شعر بيُولف بالطعنة تضرب درعه ولكنها لم تنفذ خلاله. وبسرعة استطاع بيُولف
أن ينقلب على جانبه وعندما كان يحاول الوقوف على قدميه رأى أروع سيف صنعه
الماهرون الكبار. سحبه من غمده وأتى بطرفه الحاد على أُم غرندِل.
لقد كانت ضربة نافذة لم تستطع أُم غرندِل مقاومتها فوقعت على الأرض جثة هامدة
وانغمس السيف فى دمها الشرير الساخن.

Beowulf felt the point against his armour but the blade
did not penetrate. Immediately Beowulf rolled over. As he staggered
to his feet he saw the most magnificent sword, crafted by giants.
He pulled it from its scabbard and brought the blade down upon
Grendel's mother. Such a piercing blow she could not survive and
she fell dead upon the floor.
The sword dissolved in her hot evil blood.

ونظر بيُولف حوله وشاهد الكنوز التى أكتنزها غرندِل. وكانت جثة غرندِل ترقد فى زاوية من المكان. اقترب بيُولف من جثة هذا المخلوق الشرير وقطع رأسه.

Beowulf looked around and saw the treasures that Grendel had hoarded. Lying in a corner was Grendel's corpse. Beowulf went over to the body of the evil being and hacked off Grendel's head.

حمل بيُولف رأس غرندِل ومقبض السيف بيده وعاد يسبح إلى سطح الماء حيث كان مرافقوه ينتظرونه بقلق شديد. وابتهجوا لرؤية بطلهم العظيم وساعدوه فى نزع الدرع، وامتطوا خيولهم وعادوا معه الى بلاط هيروت وهم يحملون رأس غرندِل معلّقاً على قضيب.

Holding the head and the hilt of the sword he swam to the surface of the waters where his loyal companions were anxiously waiting. They rejoiced at the sight of their great hero and helped him out of his armour. Together they rode back to Heorot carrying Grendel's head upon a pole.

وقدّم بيُولف مع مرافقيه النبلاء رأس غرندِل ومقبض السيف إلى الملك روثكار وزوجته. وألقىَ العديد من الخُطَب فى ذلك المساء. وكان بيُولف أوّل المتحدّثين، تحدّث عن قتاله الذى كاد يقضى على حياته تحت سطح الماء المتجمّد.

ثمّ جدّد روثكار شكره على كل الذى تَمَّ عمله وقال " بيُولف، أيُّها الصديق المخلص، أهِبُكَ ومرافقيكَ هذه المداليات. ستكون لكم سمعة عظيمة لتخليصنا نحن الدانماركيون من هذه المخلوقات الشريرة. لقد حان للإحتفالات أن تبدأ الآن. "

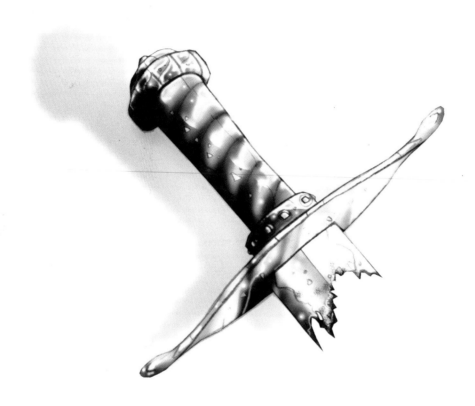

Beowulf and his fourteen noble warriors presented King Hrothgar and his queen with Grendel's head and the hilt of the sword.

There were many speeches that night. First Beowulf told of his fight and near death beneath the icy waters.

Then Hrothgar renewed his gratitude for all that had been done: "Beowulf, loyal friend, these rings I bestow upon you and your warriors. Great shall be your fame for freeing us Danes from these evil ones. Now let the celebrations begin."

وفعلاً أُقيمت الإحتفالات. واستمتع الذين احتفلوا ببلاط هيروت باكبر احتفال قط. فأكلوا
وشربوا ورقصوا واستمعوا إلى قصص القدماء. ومن تلك الليلة فصاعداً استطاع الجميع
أن ينعموا بنوم هادئ فى بيوتهم، فلم يَعُد هناك خطر ينتظرهم عِبْرَ المستنقعات.

And celebrate they did. Those gathered in Heorot had the biggest feast there had ever
been. They ate and drank, danced and listened to the tales of old. From that night forth they
all slept soundly in their beds. No longer was there a danger lurking across the marshes.

وبعد أيام قليلة استعد بيُولف ومرافقيه للعودة بحراً إلى بلادهم محمّلين بالهدايا
وقد كوّنوا صداقات بين الدانماركيين والغيتس.
وماذا حصل لبيُولف، أعظم وأنبل رجال الغيتس؟
فقد واجه مخاطر كثيرة أخرى وقاتل كثيراً من الوحوش الشريرة.
ولكن هذه قصة أخرى نقصها فى وقت آخر.

After a few days Beowulf and his men prepared to set sail for their homeland. Laden with gifts and a friendship between the Geats and the Danes they sailed away for their homes.

And what became of Beowulf, the greatest and noblest of Geats? He had many more adventures and fought many a monster.

But that is another story, to be told at another time.